THE
SHERLOCK
HOLMES

CHILDREN'S COLLECTION

SHADOWS, SECRETS AND
STOLEN TREASURE

Published by Sweet Cherry Publishing Limited
Unit 36, Vulcan House,
Vulcan Road,
Leicester, LE5 3EF
United Kingdom

First published in the UK in 2019
2019 edition

2 4 6 8 10 9 7 5 3 1

ISBN: 978-1-78226-410-1

Sherlock Holmes: The Sign of the Four

Cover Design by Arianna Bellucci and Rhiannon Izard
Illustrations by Arianna Bellucci

www.sweetcherrypublishing.com

Printed in India
I.IPP001

SHERLOCK HOLMES

THE SIGN OF THE FOUR

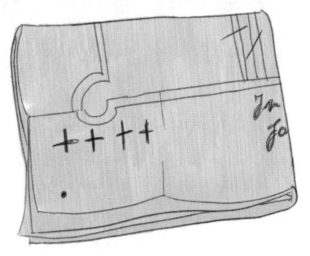

SIR ARTHUR CONAN DOYLE

Sweet Cherry
PUBLISHING

Holmes and I were talking one afternoon in our sitting room, an activity I found frustrating when he had no mystery to solve. On this particular day, he fidgeted with his pipe and complained about the lack of stimulation. I retrieved a booklet from his lap and tried to change the subject.

'What do you think of my efforts, Holmes? Did you read my account of *A Study in Scarlet*?'

'I glanced over it,' he said.

'But I cannot congratulate you. Detection is an exact science yet you have attempted to tinge it with emotion.'

I was annoyed at his criticism: my work had been specially written to please him.

'Some of my works are being translated into French,' he said, unaware of my feelings.

'Your works?'

'Oh, didn't you know?' he cried, laughing. 'I have written several small pieces. One showing the differences between more than a hundred types of tobacco and another on tracing footprints. But I bore you with my hobby.'

'Not at all,' I answered truthfully. 'Would you think me rude if I were to put your skills to the test?'

'I should be delighted to look into any problem that you might submit to me,' Holmes replied.

'I have heard you say that a person leaves their mark on any object they use regularly,' I began. As I spoke, I took a watch out of my pocket. It was not new, but it had only recently come into my possession. 'Would you have the kindness to describe the character of the previous owner of this watch?'

I handed him the watch with a slight feeling of amusement. I knew the test was impossible, and I admit that I wanted to teach him a lesson against being so certain that he was always right.

He gazed hard at the dial, opened the back, and examined the works with his magnifying glass. I could hardly keep from smiling

8

as he handed it back with a disappointed expression.

'There is hardly any data,' he said. 'The watch has been cleaned recently.'

'You are right,' I said, thinking it a poor excuse to cover his failure.

'But my research was not entirely without success,' he said, staring dreamily at the ceiling. 'I believe the watch belonged to your elder brother, who inherited it from your father.'

I nodded. 'That you gathered, no doubt, from the H. W. on the back?'

'Quite so. The
W suggests your
own name. The
watch is nearly
fifty years old, and
the initials are as old
as the watch, so it was made for
the last generation. Jewellery is
usually passed to the eldest son.
Your father has been dead many
years. It has, therefore, been in the
hands of your elder brother.'

'Right so far,' said I. 'Anything
else?'

'He was very careless. He had
all the chances he could ask

for in life, but he threw away his chances. He mostly lived in poverty with short intervals of wealth. Finally, he took to drink and died. That is all I can gather.'

I sprang from my chair and strode about the room with bitterness in my heart. 'I cannot believe that you would sink to this, Holmes. You have been asking about my poor brother, and now you pretend to deduce it from his old watch!'

'My dear Doctor,' he said kindly, 'please accept my apologies for touching on a painful subject. But

I assure you that I never even knew you had a brother until you handed me the watch.'

'Then how did you get these facts? They are absolutely correct. Was it guesswork?'

'No, no. I never guess. It seems strange to you because you do not follow my train of thought or observe the small details that lead to my deductions. I began by stating that your brother was careless. If you look at the lower part of the watch case you will notice it is marked all over. This shows he kept other hard objects, such as coins or keys, in the same pocket. A man who treats a fifty-guinea watch like that must be careless. One can also deduce that a man who inherits such a valuable object may have been well provided for in other respects.'

I nodded. My brother had inherited a large sum of money from our father.

'Pawnbrokers usually scratch the number of the ticket on the inside of the case. There are four numbers visible to my magnifying glass, so I assume he was often in financial difficulties. Then he would have times of prosperity when he could buy back the watch.

'Finally,' he said, 'look at the keyhole. Look at the thousands of scratches all around it where the key has slipped. You will never see a drunkard's watch without them. Where is the mystery in all this?'

'It is as clear as daylight,' I answered. 'I apologise. I should have had more faith in your abilities. What a pity that you have no case at present.'

I had no
sooner spoken
when, with a
crisp knock, our
landlady entered,
bearing a card on
her brass tray.

'There's a
young lady for
you, sir,' she
said, addressing
Holmes.

'Miss Mary Morstan,' he read.
'Ask the young lady to come up,
Mrs Hudson. Don't go, Doctor. I
should prefer that you remain.'

Miss Morstan entered the room with a confident manner. She was a blonde young lady, small and well-dressed. Her dress was a plain beige, and her hat was decorated with a single white feather. Her expression was sweet and her large blue eyes amiable. In all my life I have never looked upon such a refined and sensitive face.

As she took the seat that Holmes indicated, I noticed her lip tremble and her hand quiver. Her calmness hid an inner distress.

'I have come to you, Mr Holmes,'

she said, 'because of the strange situation in which I find myself.'

Holmes rubbed his hands and his eyes glistened. He leaned forward with an expression of intense concentration on his hawk-like features. 'State your case,' he said.

I felt I was intruding. 'You will excuse me,' I said, rising from my chair.

To my surprise, the young lady held up her hand. 'If your friend would be good enough to stay, he might be of great service to me.'

I sat back down.

'My father was an officer in an Indian regiment, and he sent me home when I was a child,' Miss Morstan began. 'My mother died when I was young and I had no relatives in England, so I was placed in a residence in Edinburgh until I was seventeen. In 1878 my father came home. He telegraphed me from London, saying that he had arrived safely and was staying at the Langham Hotel. I travelled to London and drove to the Langham. There I was informed that Captain Morstan *was* staying there but had gone out the night before and hadn't returned. I waited all day and called the police that evening, when he had still not returned. I placed an advert in all the papers, but from that day no word has ever been heard of my father …' A choking sob cut short her sentence.

'The date?' asked Holmes, opening his notebook.

'He disappeared on the third of December, 1878 – nearly ten years ago.'

'His luggage?'

'At the hotel. There were some books, clothes and a few curiosities from the Andaman Islands. He had been one of the officers in charge of the convicts there.'

'Did he know anyone in London?'

'Only one person that I know of: Major Sholto, who was in the same regiment. He retired some time before and lived in Upper Norwood. He did not even know that my father had returned to England.'

'A strange case,' mused Holmes.

'But the strangest part is this,' went on Miss Morstan. 'In May 1882 an advertisement appeared in *The Times* asking for my address and stating that it would be to my advantage to come forwards. At that time I had just begun working for Mrs Forrester

The Times
2nd May 1882

as a governess. On her advice I
published my address, and the
same day a small cardboard box
arrived in the post, containing a
very large pearl. There was no note.
Since then, every year on the same
date I receive a similar pearl with
no clue about the sender. The pearls
are rare and valuable. You can see
for yourself.'

She opened a flat box as she

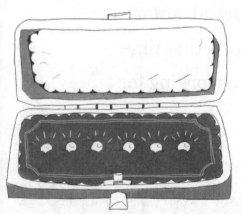

spoke and
showed us six
of the finest
pearls I had
ever seen.

'Most interesting,' said Holmes. 'Is there anything else?'

'Yes. This morning I received a letter,' she said, handing a neat envelope to Holmes.

Be at the third pillar from the left outside the Lyceum Theatre tonight at seven o'clock. If you are distrustful, bring two friends. You are a wronged woman and shall have justice. Do not bring police. If you do, all will be in vain.

Your unknown friend

'Well, this is a pretty little mystery, Miss Morstan. What do you intend to do?'

'That is exactly what I want to ask you about.'

'Then we shall most certainly go. Doctor Watson is the best man to accompany us. He and I have worked together before.'

'I shall be very glad to come along,' I said.

'You are both kind,' replied the young lady. 'I have no friends whom I could ask. Shall I be here at six?'

'And no later,' said Holmes. 'May

I see the pearl boxes?'

He compared the note with the box. 'Your mystery person has disguised his handwriting on all but the letter, but they are undoubtedly by the same person. Not your father's writing I suppose?'

'Nothing could be less like it.'

'Thank you, Miss Morstan. We shall expect you here at six o' clock.'

With a kindly glance from one to the other of us, she put away the pearl box and left. Standing by the window, I watched her walk briskly down the street until her grey hat and white feather were lost in the crowd.

'What an attractive woman!' I exclaimed.

Holmes had lit his pipe and was leaning back in his chair. 'Is she?' he said. 'I did not observe.'

'You are not human!' I cried.

He smiled gently. 'It is important not to let your judgement be influenced by personal qualities. The most charming woman I ever knew was hanged for poisoning three little children for their insurance money.'

'But in this case ...'

'I never make exceptions. Have you ever studied handwriting? What do you make of this fellow's scribble?'

I glanced at it. 'It's neat,' I offered.

Holmes shook his head and rose from his chair. 'I shall be back in an hour.'

I nodded absentmindedly. My mind was on our visitor: her smile, her voice, the strange mystery that surrounded her.

If she was seventeen when her father disappeared she must be twenty-seven now. Such a sweet age. I realised that I was becoming fond of her and I hurried away to my desk to read some medical articles.

Holmes returned at around five-thirty. He was in an excellent mood, almost bouncing into the room.

Mrs Hudson had brought up some tea and I poured him a cup.

'There is no great mystery here,' he said, taking the tea and sitting opposite me at the table. 'The facts show only one explanation.'

'What! Have you solved it already?'

'Well, I can't go as far as that, but I have discovered an important fact. I looked into the back files of *The Times* and discovered that Major Sholto died on the twenty-eighth of April, 1882.'

'I may be a bit dim, Holmes, but I fail to see what this suggests.'

28th April 188

The Times.

Obituary
Major Sholto
We announce the death of Major James Sholto on the 28ᵗʰ of April ....ed had retired

Holmes raised his eyebrows. 'No? You surprise me. Look at it this way. Captain Morstan disappears. The only person in London he could have visited is Major Sholto, who denied seeing him. Four years later Sholto dies. Within a week of his death Captain Morstan's daughter receives a valuable present, which is repeated every year. Now a letter arrives describing her as a wronged woman. What wrong can it refer to? The loss of her father? And why should the presents begin immediately after Sholto's death unless his heir knows something of the mystery and wants to put things right?'

'What a strange way of putting things right,' I said. 'And why should he write a letter now and not six years ago? And what justice? Could her father be alive?'

'We shall see tonight,' said Holmes, standing up and going to the window. 'Ah, here is the cab with Miss Morstan inside. Are you ready? It's past the hour. Please bring your revolver.'

I grabbed my coat and hat and followed Holmes.

Miss Morstan was wrapped in a dark cloak. Her sensitive face was pale but calm. She must have felt some unease, yet she had a way of not showing it.

'Major Sholto was a close friend of Father's,' she said, in answer to a question from Holmes. 'Father mentioned him often in letters. They commanded the troops in the Andaman Islands together. By the way, a curious paper was found in Father's desk. No one could understand it.' She took a folded paper from her bag and handed it to Holmes, who opened it carefully and spread it on his knee so as to catch some light.

'The paper was made in India,' he said. 'It has been pinned to a board at some point. The diagram appears to be a plan of a large building with many corridors. There is a small cross in red ink. In the left hand corner is a strange mark like four crosses in a line, with their arms touching. Beside it, in very rough writing, it says: "The sign of the four – Jonathan Small, Mahomet Singh, Abdullah Khan, Dost Akbar."'

Holmes looked up. 'It must have

been important for him to take such care of it. Keep it safe, Miss Morstan, for it may prove useful.'

Holmes leaned back in his seat and I could see that he was deep in thought. Meanwhile, Miss Morstan and I chatted quietly.

Although it was not yet seven o'clock, the day had been dreary and a dense fog lay over the city. The yellow glare from the shop windows threw a murky light across the crowded street and the people we saw looked eerie and ghost-like.

This atmosphere made me feel quite nervous and I could see that Miss Morstan felt the same. Only Holmes did not seem to be affected. He held his open notebook on his knee, from time to time jotting things down in it.

At the Lyceum Theatre, crowds

were already thick. A continuous stream of Hansom cabs and four-wheelers rattled up, let out their finely dressed passengers, and went on their way.

We had hardly reached the third pillar when a small man dressed as a coachman hailed us.

'Are you the people who come with Miss Morstan?' he asked.

'I am Miss Morstan and these are my two gentlemen friends,' she said.

He looked her directly in the eye.

'You will excuse me, Miss, but you must give me your word that neither of your companions is a police officer.'

'I give you my word,' she replied.

He gave a shrill whistle. A boy led a cab in front of us and opened the door. The man who had addressed us climbed up into the driver's seat while we took our places inside. Then he whipped up the horse and we plunged at a furious pace through the foggy streets.

I like to think that I have a decent knowledge of London but as we moved beyond the centre I found myself unable to recognise our location. Holmes had no such problem and he muttered the names of the streets as the cab rattled on.

'Rochester Row,' he said. 'Now Vincent Square. Now we're on the Vauxhall Bridge Road and about to cross the river. Yes, we're on the bridge now.

'Wordsworth Road,' he went on, 'Priory Road, Lark Hill Lane, Stockwell Place, Robert Street,

Cold Harbour Lane. Our quest does not take us to fashionable areas.'

It was indeed a neighbourhood of dull brick houses relieved only by the occasional inn.

At last our cab drew up at the third house in a new terrace. The houses were dark and uninhabited, except the one at which we stopped, which had a single glimmer from one window.

Holmes knocked and the door was immediately thrown open by a servant clad in a yellow turban and white loose-fitting clothes.

'The sahib awaits you,' he said.

'Show them in to me,' said a high, piping voice from inside.

We followed the man down a shabby, poorly lit passage until he came to a door, which he flung open. A blaze of yellow light streamed out, and in the centre of the glare stood a small man with a bristle of red hair in a fringe around his head and a bald shining scalp in the centre.

He seemed anxious, wringing his hands nervously one minute, smiling the next.

'Your servant, Miss Morstan, gentlemen,' he said, in the same thin, high voice. 'Please step into my sanctum.'

We were all surprised at the appearance of the apartment. Two great tiger skins were spread out on the floor and a lamp in the shape of a silver dove hung on a golden wire in the centre of the room. As it burned, it filled the air with a pleasant aroma.

'Mr Thaddeus Sholto,' said the little man, smiling. 'And you are Miss Morstan, of course, and these gentlemen–'

'This is Mr Sherlock Holmes and Doctor Watson.'

'I am glad to have your friends here. The three of us can face my brother, Bartholomew, and we can settle everything amongst ourselves without any interference.' He sat down on a low settee.

'For my part,' said Holmes, 'whatever you say will go no further.'

I nodded to show my agreement.

'That is well. May I offer you a glass of wine, Miss Morstan? No? Very well.' Sholto shifted on his settee and began his explanation.

'When I first contacted you, I could have given you my address, but I feared that you might bring unpleasant people with you. I sent my man, Williams, to see you first. You will forgive all these precautions, but I rarely come in contact with the rough crowd. I live with an atmosphere of elegance around me. I call myself a patron of the arts, and I am–'

'You will excuse me, Mr Sholto,' said Miss Morstan. 'But I am here to learn something you desire to tell me. It is very late and I want my visit to be as short as possible.'

'It will take some time,' he said, 'for we must go to Norwood to see my brother, Bartholomew. He is very angry at me for contacting you, so it would hardly do to bring you suddenly. No, I must prepare you by telling you all I know.'

We settled ourselves for a long session.

'My father was Major John Sholto, once of the Indian Army,' he began, puffing on his pipe.

'He retired eleven years ago and went to live in Pondicherry Lodge in Upper Norwood. He had prospered in India and brought back with him a large sum of money, a large collection of valuable items and a staff of Indian servants. My twin brother and I were his only children.

I remember the disappearance of Captain Morstan. We read the details in the papers and discussed it with him. Never did we suspect that he alone knew what had happened to Arthur Morstan.'

I saw Miss Morstan shudder at the mention of her father's name and placed a comforting arm around her shoulder. She leaned against me.

Thaddeus Sholto continued his story. 'We did know that there was some mystery about our father. He was afraid to go out alone and always employed two boxers to act as porters at Pondicherry Lodge. He also had a fear of men with wooden legs. He once shot at a wooden-legged man, who turned out to be a harmless tradesman. We had to pay a large sum to hush the matter up.

Early in 1882 my father received a letter from India that

nearly caused him to faint. From
that day onwards he took ill and
never recovered. We went to see
him on his deathbed, propped up
and breathing heavily. He asked
us to lock the doors and said in
a broken voice, "I have one thing
that weighs on my mind and it

is the treatment of Morstan's orphan. My greed has deprived her of at least half of the treasure that should have been hers. I have made no use of it myself. I could not bear to share it. After I have gone, you will give her a fair share of the Agra treasure."'

Sholto looked at Miss Morstan. 'He told us how your father died. He had suffered for years from a weak heart, but he never told anyone. While in India, he and my father came into possession of a considerable treasure, which Father brought here to England.

On the night of Morstan's arrival, he came over to collect his share but he and Father quarrelled about how to divide it. Morstan sprang from his chair in anger, but suddenly grasped his side, fell backwards and struck his head on a corner of the treasure chest. My father said that when he bent over him, Morstan was dead.'

Miss Morstan began to weep and I offered her my handkerchief. Sholto paused for a moment before continuing.

'My father did not know what to do. He could be accused of murder.

The quarrel and the gash on the head would work against him, and he could not reveal what the argument was about. His servant came in at that moment and, thinking my father had done the deed, offered to take care of the body. After Father finished telling us this sad tale he said, "Listen closely. The treasure is hidden in–"

At that instant, a horrible change came over his expression. He stared wildly and he yelled in a voice that I shall never forget, "Keep him out! For heaven's sake, keep him out!"

'We both turned to look at the window and a face was looking in at us, its nose pressed against the glass.  It was a bearded, hairy face, with wild eyes and an expression of pure evil. My brother and I rushed to the window but the man had gone. When we turned back to my father he was dead.'

There was silence. Sholto took a deep breath and continued.

'We searched the garden but

found no proof that anyone had been there except for a single footprint under the window. The next morning we found that my father's room had been broken into, though nothing seemed to have been stolen. Fixed to his chest was a note that said *The sign of the four*. I have no idea what the phrase meant and it is still a mystery to us.'

Miss Morstan was pale and gladly took the water I offered her. Holmes sat back in his chair with a vacant look in his eyes and I thought that here, at last, he was faced with solving a problem that would challenge him.

'My brother and I,' Thaddeus Sholto went on, 'were excited about the treasure. For months we dug in every part of the garden without discovering it. It was maddening to think that he had been about to reveal its hiding place at the moment of his death. We did have a string of pearls though, and I persuaded my brother that we should send Miss Morstan a pearl at regular

intervals so that she may still benefit.'

'It was a kindly thought,' said Miss Morstan.

Sholto waved his hand. 'It was our duty. That was the way I thought of it anyway. But we did have a difference of opinion over it, and I decided to move out of Pondicherry Lodge. Yesterday I learned that the treasure has been discovered. Now it only remains for us to drive to Pondicherry Lodge and demand our share.

We shall be expected, if not welcome, visitors.'

Holmes was the first to spring to his feet. 'You have done well, sir. It is possible that we may have some answers to events that you know nothing about, but it is late. Let us go without delay.'

Our friend reached for a heavy coat, which he put on and buttoned up to the collar, despite the mild night. I raised an eyebrow. 'My health is fragile,' he explained, and led us to the cab waiting outside.

Sholto talked non-stop as we rattled along. 'Bartholomew is

a clever fellow. He realised that the treasure must be somewhere in the house so he measured the building and discovered that there was a space that didn't appear in the plans. He knocked a hole in the ceiling of the bedroom and discovered an attic that had been sealed up. In the centre stood a treasure chest resting on two rafters, so he lowered it through the hole into his bedroom. He estimated the value of the jewels to be over half a million pounds.'

At the mention of this gigantic sum we stared at one another, wide-eyed. Miss Morstan would become one of the richest women in the country. I felt that I should rejoice with her, but I am ashamed to say that I saw it as a barrier between us. Sholto babbled on for the rest of the journey and I was relieved when we stopped and the cabman opened the door.

'This, Miss Morstan, is Pondicherry Lodge,' said Mr Thaddeus Sholto as he helped her out.

It was nearly eleven o'clock. Heavy clouds moved across the sky with the moon occasionally

peeping through. Thaddeus
Sholto took down one of the
carriage lamps to light our way
and we started towards the single
iron door to the house, which
stood surrounded by a high stone
wall topped with broken glass.
He knocked.

'Who is there?' called a gruff
voice from within.

'It is I, McMurdo.'

There was a grumbling sound
and a clanking of keys. Then the
heavy door swung back and a
short, broad-chested porter stood
in the doorway.

'I can let you in, but I have no orders about these others,' he said.

'But I told my brother last night that I should bring friends.'

'I have no orders.'

'The young lady cannot wait out on a public road at this hour.'

'Very sorry, Mr Thaddeus,' said the porter. 'The master pays me well to do my duty, and my duty I'll do. I don't know none of your friends.'

'Oh, yes, you do, McMurdo,' cried Holmes. 'I don't think you can have forgotten me, the amateur who fought three rounds with you four years back?'

'Not Mr Sherlock Holmes!'
cried the prize-fighter. 'How could
I have mistook you? You could
have just given me that cross-hit of
yours across the jaw and I'd have
known you without question! You
have wasted gifts, you have.'

'You see, Watson, If all else fails I still have a profession open to me,' said Holmes, laughing.

'In you come, sir, in you come, and your friends.'

We crossed a courtyard to the huge house. It was completely dark except where a moonbeam glimmered on an attic window. Its deathly silence struck a chill to the heart.

'I do not understand it,' said Sholto. 'I told Bartholomew we were coming yet there is no light in the window.' The lantern quivered in his hand.

'I see a glint of light in that little window beside the door,' said Holmes.

'That is the housekeeper's room. Perhaps you wouldn't mind waiting for a moment–'

From the great black house came a pitiful sound – a shrill and broken whimpering. Miss Morstan seized my wrist and we all stood with thumping hearts, straining our ears.

'It is Mrs Bernstone,' said Sholto. 'Wait here.'

He hurried towards the door and a tall woman opened it for

him. 'Oh, Mr Thaddeus, sir, I'm so glad you've come!' Then the door closed and we heard no more.

Sholto had left us the lantern. Holmes swung it round slowly and peered around the grounds. Miss Morstan and I stood together and her hand was in mine. What a wonderful thing love is, for we had never seen each other before that day, and yet in our hour of trouble our hands sought each other.

'What a strange place,' said Miss Morstan. 'It looks as though all

the moles in England have been let loose in it'.

'These are the traces of the treasure-seekers,' Holmes replied in a low whisper. Remember that they spent six years looking for it.'

At that moment the door of the house burst open, and Thaddeus Sholto came running out with terror in his eyes.

'There is something wrong with Bartholomew!' he cried.

'Come into the house,' said Holmes firmly.

We followed him into the housekeeper's room. The old woman was pacing up and down.

'God bless you for coming!' she cried with a hysterical sob. 'It has been a terrible day and now the master has locked himself in his room. An hour ago I feared that something was wrong and I went up and peeped through the keyhole. You must go up, Mr Thaddeus, and see for yourself. I have seen Mr Bartholomew in joy and sorrow for ten long years, but I never saw him with such a face on him as that!'

Miss Morstan stayed behind with the frightened housekeeper. Holmes took the lamp and led the way. Sholto was so shaken that I had to assist him up the stairs.

Once we had reached the third floor Holmes continued in his slow, methodical way along the passage and we kept close behind him, our long black shadows streaming behind us. Holmes knocked and tried the handle, but it was locked from the inside. Finally he bent, held the light to the keyhole, and peered through. Then he gasped and stood up.

'There is something devilish in this, Watson.'

I kneeled down to the hole and recoiled in horror. Moonlight streamed into the room and lit up a figure sitting in the chair. It was the face of our acquaintance,

Thaddeus Sholto. This face, however, had a fixed and unnatural grin upon it. I remembered that Thaddeus had a twin.

'This is terrible!' I cried. 'But what do we do?'

'The door must come down,' Holmes said gravely. Together we flung our shoulders against it. It creaked and groaned, then finally gave way with a snap.

The room was fitted out as a laboratory with Bunsen burners, test tubes and containers of acid on the shelves. One of these containers had leaked and a dark liquid that smelled of tar was dripping onto the floor. At one side of the room, a set of steps stood amongst a pile of plaster and above that was a hole in the ceiling. A long rope was piled in a careless heap nearby.

Sholto's brother had not moved, and as I got closer I saw that he was dead. On the table beside him sat a peculiar instrument – a brown stick with a stone head like a hammer lashed with coarse string. Beside it was a torn sheet of notepaper with some words scrawled on it. Holmes glanced at it and then handed it to me.

In the light of the lantern I read

with a thrill of horror: *The sign of the four*.

'What does it mean?'

'It means murder,' said Holmes, leaning over the body. 'Ah! Look here!'

He pointed to a dark object stuck just above Bartholomew's ear.

'It looks like a thorn,' I said.

'It is a thorn. You may pick it out, but be careful. It is poisoned.'

I carefully removed it and wrapped it in my handkerchief. 'This is all a mystery to me and becomes more so all the time.'

'On the contrary,' said Holmes. 'It becomes clearer to me. Only a few more missing links and I shall have solved the case.'

We had almost forgotten our companion's presence. Sholto was still standing in the doorway. Suddenly he gave a sharp cry.

'The treasure is gone! I was the last person to see him. I left him here last night and I heard him lock the door!'

'What time was that?'

'It was ten o'clock. And now he is dead. The police will be called and I shall be suspected of killing him! Would I have brought you here if I were guilty? Oh dear! Oh dear!'

'You have no reason to fear, Mr Sholto,' said Holmes kindly, putting his hand on the quivering shoulder. 'Drive down to the police station and report the matter. We shall wait here until you return.'

Looking stunned, the little man obeyed and we heard him stumbling down the stairs in the dark.

'Now, Watson,' said Holmes, rubbing his hands. 'We have half an hour to ourselves. Let us make good use of it. My case is almost complete but I must not be over-confident. Simple as it seems, there may be something deeper behind it.'

'Simple!' I cried.

'Of course,' he said, with an expression of superiority. 'Now, how did these folk get in? The door has not been opened since last night. How is the window?' He examined it closely. 'It is closed from the inside. The framework is solid.' Throwing the window open, Holmes nodded. 'Yes, a man has entered by the window. Here is a footprint on the sill. And here is

a circular muddy mark, and here
again on the floor, and again by
the table!'

'That is not a footprint,' I said,
puzzled.

'It is something much more
valuable. It is the impression of a
wooden leg.'

'It is the wooden-legged man.'

'Quite so. But there is someone
else – someone very able and agile.
Could you scale that wall, Doctor?'

I looked out of the open window. We were a good sixty feet from the ground and, no matter where I looked, I could not see any possible foothold in the brickwork. 'It is absolutely impossible.'

'Without help it is, but if you had a friend up here who lowered you a good strong rope like that one there on the floor, then I think you could climb up, wooden leg and all. You would depart, of course, by the same way, and your friend would close the window and leave in the way he originally came. By the way,' he continued, 'our wooden-legged friend was not a sailor. My magnifying glass shows blood on the rope caused by his rapid descent, which took the skin off his hands.'

'What about this mysterious friend?' I asked. 'How did he enter? Did he come down the chimney?'

Holmes shook his head. 'It is too small. I have often said that when you have eliminated the impossible, whatever remains, however improbable, must be the truth. What else is there?'

'He came through the hole in the roof!' I cried.

'Of course he did. If you would be good enough to hold the lamp for me, we will continue our search in the room above.'

He mounted the steps, seized a

rafter with each hand, and swung himself up into the attic. Then he held the lamp while I followed.

The floor of the small room was formed of rafters with only the plaster ceiling between, so we had to step from beam to beam.

'Here you are, you see,' said Holmes, putting his hand against the sloping wall. 'This is a trapdoor that leads out onto the roof. This is the way that he entered.'

He then shone the lamp onto the floor. In the dust there were clear prints of a naked foot roughly half the size of a man's.

'Holmes, a child has done this thing.'

Irritation flashed across his face. 'My memory failed me, or I would have been able to predict this. There is nothing more to be learned here. Let us go down.'

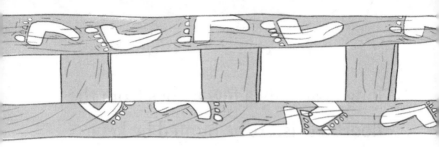

'What is your theory then, as to the footmarks?' I asked once we had returned to the bedroom.

'My dear Watson, try a little analysis yourself,' he said, a little impatiently. 'You know my methods.'

'I cannot think of anything that fits the facts.'

'It will be clear enough to you soon,' he said. He reached into his pocket, produced his magnifying glass and tape measure, and then began examining the room, with his long nose only a few inches from the floorboards. As he hunted he kept muttering to himself, and finally he broke out into a loud crow of delight.

'We are in luck,' he said. 'This person has been unlucky enough to tread in creosote from that leaking container. I know a dog that would follow that scent to the end of the end of the world – but, hello, here are the police.'

We could hear heavy steps and loud voices from below. The front door shut with a crash.

'Before they come,' said Holmes. 'What do you make of

the unnatural expression on the poor man's face?'

'Death from some powerful poison,' I said.

'Exactly,' said Holmes. 'That's why I looked for a clue a soon as I entered the room. Do you have that thorn?'

I opened my handkerchief and carefully held up the thorn. It was long, sharp and black with some gummy substance on the tip.

'Is it an English thorn?' Holmes asked, already knowing my answer.

'It certainly is not,' I replied.

As I spoke, a portly man with grey hair strode heavily into the room. He was red-faced and burly, with a pair of small twinkly eyes that looked out from between puffy cheeks. A police officer and Thaddeus Sholto began to follow him into the room until he dismissed them both with a wave of his hand.

'Why, the house seems as full as a rabbit warren,' he boomed.

'I think you know me, Mr Athelney Jones,' said Holmes, quietly.

'Why, of course I do! You set us on the right track in the Bishopsgate jewellery case, but you must admit that it was more good luck than good guidance.'

'It was a piece of very simple reasoning.'

'Oh, come now, never be ashamed of owning up. But what is all this? Door locked, I understand. Jewels worth half a million missing. How was the window?'

'Fastened, but there were steps on the sill.'

'Well, if it was fastened, the steps on the sill must have nothing to do with it. Ha! I have a theory. What do you think of this, Holmes? Thaddeus Sholto was with his brother last night. His brother died in a fit and Sholto walked off with the treasure.'

'After which, the dead man got up and locked the door.'

I chuckled.

'Hm. There is a flaw there. Well, no one saw the brother after

Thaddeus left him. He is in a disturbed state of mind. You see that I am weaving a web around Thaddeus. The net begins to close in upon him.'

'You do not have all the facts yet,' said Holmes, picking up the thorn from the table. 'I believe this thorn to be poisoned. It was in the victim's scalp, and this paper was on the table next to this curious stone-headed hammer. How does that fit your theory?'

'Confirms it,' said the detective. 'The house is full of Indian curiosities. Thaddeus may well have used it. The note is to put us on the wrong track. The only question is, how did he leave? Ah, the hole in the roof of course.'

I was surprised at how easily he went up the steps and climbed through the hole. Then came a cry of glee as he discovered the trapdoor.

Holmes looked at me and shrugged. 'He can find something.'

Athelney Jones came back down the steps. 'You see!' he said. 'There is a trapdoor out onto the roof and it is partly open.'

'It was I who opened it.'

'Oh, you noticed it then?'
For a moment Jones seemed disappointed but he recovered and shouted for the officer. The policeman and Sholto rushed into the room.

Jones spoke to Thaddeus, but fixed his glare on Holmes. 'Mr Sholto, I am arresting you for the murder of your brother, Mr Bartholomew Sholto. Anything you say may be used against you.'

'Didn't I tell you?' cried the little man, throwing out his hands and looking from one to the other of us.

'Don't trouble yourself, Mr Sholto,' said Holmes. 'I can clear you of the charge.'

'Don't promise too much,' said Athelney Jones.

'Not only will I clear him, Mr Jones, but I will tell you the name and description of one of the two men who were in this room last night. He is Mr Jonathan Small. He's a poorly educated man, small, active and with an amputated right leg replaced by a wooden one, which is worn away on the inside. His left boot has a square-toed sole with an iron band around the heel. He is a middle-aged man, much sunburned, and has been a convict. There is a good deal of skin missing from the palms of his hands.'

I could not help chuckling at the expressions of disbelief on the faces of the policemen.

'And the other man?' sneered Jones.

'I hope, before long, to be able to introduce you to the pair of them.' Holmes led me out of the room and onto the landing. 'Miss Morstan cannot remain in this house. Please take her home, Watson. She lives with Mrs Cecil Forrester in Lower Camberwell. It's not very far. I will wait for you here, unless you are too tired?'

'By no means,' I said. 'I don't think I can rest until I know more about this strange business. I would like to see the matter through.'

'Your presence will be of great service to me,' he answered.

'When you have dropped off Miss Morstan, go to Number 3, Pinchin Lane, down near the water's edge at Lambeth. The house belongs to a taxidermist called Sherman. Wake him up and tell him that I want Toby at once. You will bring Toby back in the cab with you.'

'A dog, I suppose?'

'Yes, one with a most amazing sense of smell. I would rather have Toby's help than the whole detective force of London.'

'It is one o'clock now. I ought to be back before three.'

'And I,' said Holmes, 'shall

see what I can learn from Mrs Bernstone and the servant.'

The police had brought a cab with them, and in this I escorted Miss Morstan home. I had found her calmly comforting the housekeeper, but once we were in the cab, she burst into tears. I longed to comfort her but I held back. She had suffered unpleasant experiences from which she needed to recover. What's more, she was to be a rich heiress while I was only a poor surgeon on sick pay. The treasure was like a barrier between us.

Although it was nearly two o'clock when we reached Mrs Forrester's, the good lady had waited up and welcomed Miss Morstan with a tender arm around her shoulders. Miss Morstan was clearly more of a friend than a paid governess. I promised them

I would report any news. As we drove away, I looked back at the two figures in the doorway.

Pinchin Lane was a row of shabby brick houses in Lambeth. I had to knock for some time at Number 3 before I could wake anyone. At last there was the glint of a candle and a face looked out of the window.

'Go on, you vagabond, or I'll set all forty-three dogs on you!'

'But I want a dog!' I cried. 'I've been sent by Mr Sherlock Holmes–'

The words had a magical effect and the window was slammed

down. Within a minute the door was opened. Mr Sherman was a lanky, lean old man with stooping shoulders and blue-tinted glasses.

'A friend of Mr Sherlock Holmes is always welcome,' he said. 'Come in.'

I asked the cabby to wait, stepped inside and followed Sherman as he moved forward with his candle among the strange animal family that he had gathered around him.

In the shadowy light I could see eyes peeping down from every corner.

'My apologies for being a little short with you. I'm plagued with children who come down this lane just to wake me up. What was it that Mr Sherlock Holmes wanted, sir?'

'He wanted a dog of yours.'

'Ah, that would be Toby. He's over here.'

Toby proved to be a long-haired, lop-eared creature, half spaniel and half lurcher. He was brown and white in colour and had a very clumsy way of walking. He accepted, with some hesitation, a lump of sugar that his owner gave me and then seemed happy to follow me to the cab.

It was just after three o' clock when we arrived back at Pondicherry Lodge. The police officers at the gate let me in and I found Holmes standing on the doorstep with his hands in his pockets.

'Ah, you have him!' he said. 'Good dog! Athelney Jones has

gone. He arrested Thaddeus, the
gatekeeper, the housekeeper and
the servant. Leave the dog here
and come upstairs.'

I tied the dog to the hall table
and followed him.

'Now,' said Holmes, 'I must take
off my socks and boots. I am going
to do a little climbing. Come with
me into the attic, Watson.'

We clambered up through the
hole and Holmes shone the light
on the footprints. 'Do you notice
anything unusual about them?'

'They belong to a child or a
woman,' I said.

'Apart from the size, anything else?'

I shook my head.

Holmes planted his bare foot beside it. 'Now, do you see any difference?'

'Your toes are all cramped together. In the other print each toe is separate.'

'Quite so. Now, would you kindly step over to the trapdoor and smell the edge of the woodwork?'

I did so, and was instantly aware of a strong tarry smell.

'That is where he put his foot

when he was getting out. Toby
should have no trouble finding
him. Run downstairs, let the dog
off his lead, and look out for me.'

By the time I got out to the
grounds Holmes was crawling very
slowly along the ridge of the roof.
I lost sight of his lantern behind a
stack of chimneys but when I went
round to the other side, I found him
sitting by one of the corner eaves.

'Any sign of a ladder, Watson?'

'No.'

'Curse the fellow! I ought to
be able to come down where he
climbed up. This water pipe feels

pretty firm. Here goes.'

My heart was in my mouth as I watched him come steadily down the wall. I was amazed at Holmes' many abilities. Violin playing, boxing and now climbing down a wall at night, without any specialist equipment.

With a light spring, he landed on a water barrel and climbed down onto the ground.

'It was easy following him,' he said as he put on his socks and boots. 'Tiles were loosened all along and in his hurry he dropped this.'

He held up a small pouch woven out of grasses. Inside were half a dozen thorns like the one that we had found in Bartholomew Sholto's scalp.

'These are hellish things,' he said. 'But I'm glad we have

found them. Chances are it's all he has so we shall not find one in our skin. Are you up for a six-mile walk, Watson?'

'Certainly,' I answered, surprised that it was actually true. This mystery was stimulating.

'Here you are, doggy. Smell it, Toby.' He pushed a creosote-soaked handkerchief under the dog's nose while it stood and tilted its head comically. Holmes then fastened a strong cord to the dog's collar and led him to the foot of the water barrel. Toby instantly gave a few high yelps and, with his nose to the ground, set off at top speed.

Dawn was breaking as we reached the boundary wall, where Toby ran along, whining, and finally stopped in a corner. Where the two walls joined, several bricks had been loosened. Holmes clambered up, took the dog from me, dropped him on the other side.

'There's the print of Wooden-leg's hand,' he remarked as I climbed up beside him. 'You see the blood on the stone here. What a lucky thing that we've had no rain since yesterday! The scent will lie on the road despite their twenty-eight hour start.'

I had some doubts, considering all the traffic that had passed along the streets in that time, but Toby never hesitated or swerved. Instead he waddled along in his peculiar fashion, never distracted from the scent.

'Do not think,' said Holmes, 'that I depended on this fellow stepping in the creosote. I have enough knowledge of the case to be able to trace them in other ways, but this is the easiest.'

'Holmes, I marvel at the means

by which you obtain your results. How, for example, could you describe the man with the wooden leg with such confidence?'

'It is simplicity itself! Two officers in charge of a prison learn about some buried treasure. An Englishman called Jonathan Small draws a map for them. You remember we saw the name on Morstan's chart. He signed it on behalf of himself and his associates – the sign of the four, as he dramatically called it. Aided by the chart, one of the officers got the treasure and brought it

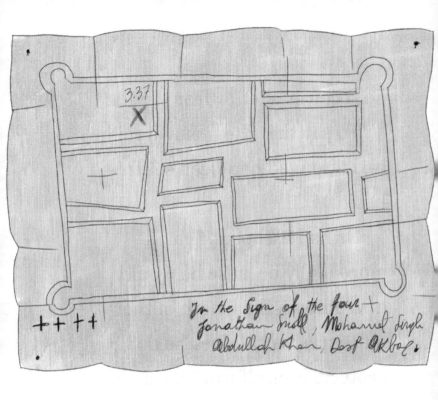

back to England. Now, why didn't
Jonathan Small get the treasure
himself? The answer is obvious.
Jonathan Small and the others
were prisoners. Major Sholto
remains happily in possession of
the treasure for several years until

he receives a letter from India.'

'To say that the men whom he had wronged had been set free,' I said.

'Or had escaped. That is more likely because he would have known the length of their sentences. What does he do? He protects himself from a wooden-legged man – an Englishman, since he once mistook a trader for him. He is the only Englishman whose name appeared on the map. So the wooden-legged man must be Jonathan Small. Is that clear?'

'Clear and concise,' said I.

'Let us put ourselves in the place of Jonathan Small. He comes to England to claim his share of the treasure and have his revenge on the person who had wronged him. He finds out where Sholto lives but cannot locate the treasure. Then he hears that the major is on his deathbed. He runs to the window and is only prevented from entering by the two sons. Small later enters the room and searches the major's papers in the hope of finding a clue to where the treasure lies.'

'Unsuccessfully.'

'Quite so. But he leaves the note on the body. Much later, through some informant within the household, he hears of the discovery of the attic and the treasure within. But how is he to climb up with his wooden leg? He brings with him an assistant who is able to do the climb, but this fellow accidentally dips his foot in the creosote and leaves a trail for Toby to follow.'

'So it was the assistant and not

Jonathan who committed the crime.'

'Yes,' said Holmes. 'Jonathan bore no grudge against Bartholomew Sholto and would have preferred him tied up rather than killed. But the poison dart had done its work so all he could do was to lower the treasure chest to the ground and follow it himself. As to his appearance, he must be middle-aged and sunburned after serving his time in the Andaman Islands. I calculated his height by the length of his stride, and we know that he was bearded because Thaddeus Sholto saw him at the window.'

'And the assistant?'

'Ah, there's no great mystery in that,' he replied mildly. Suddenly he became very serious and fixed me with an intense look. 'Do you have your revolver?'

I nodded and hoped it wouldn't be needed.

We had now reached the outskirts of the city. Labourers and dockmen were up and about. But despite the other dogs around,

Toby continued on his mission, nose to the ground.

We were soon in the heart of London. When we got to Miles Place, Toby began running back and forth uncertainly. Then he waddled round in circles, looking at us from time to time as if asking for sympathy.

'What on earth is wrong with the dog?' growled Holmes. 'They surely would not take a cab or go off in a balloon.'

'Perhaps they stood here for some time.'

'Ah, he is off again.'

The scent was stronger than before, judging by the pace he kept. We ran to keep up with him, and I barely had time to smile at the thought of Sherlock Holmes struggling to keep up for once.

At last we hurried down Nine Elms into a timber yard where the sawyers were already hard at work. The dog raced through the sawdust, down an alley, between two wood piles, and finally, with a triumphant yelp, sprang upon a large barrel. With lolling tongue and blinking eyes, Toby looked at us. The outside of the barrel was smeared with dark liquid and the air was heavy with the smell of creosote.

Holmes and I burst into an uncontrollable fit of laughter.

Holmes lifted Toby down from the barrel. 'If you consider how much creosote is

carted about London every day, it's no wonder our trail should have been crossed.'

'Evidently what puzzled the dog at the corner of Miles Place was the two trails running in opposite directions,' I said.

We led Toby back to where he had been unsure. He sniffed about for a moment before dashing off in a different direction.

'We must take care that he does not take us to the place where the creosote barrel came from,' I said.

'I had thought of that, but you will notice that he keeps on the

pavement. The barrel passed
down the road. We are on the right
track now.'

We went down towards the
river. At the end of Broad Street
the trail ran right to a small
wooden wharf at the water's edge.
There Toby stood whining, looking
out across the water.

'We are out of luck,' said Holmes. 'They have taken a boat here.'

Close to the wharf was a small house with a sign in the window saying: *Mordecai Smith, Boats to hire by the hour or day*. Another sign said that a steam launch was available.

Steam launch

Fast little wooden boats. Very popular on the Thames. Thousands of people use them to get to work each day, and to take pleasure trips to Southend. They are often paddle steamers with a paddle wheel either side and a funnel in the centre. Between twenty and forty feet in length.

'These fellows are cleverer than I expected,' Holmes sighed. As he approached the door, it opened and a lad of about six ran out followed by a red-faced woman with a large sponge in her hand.

'You come and be washed, Jack! Your father will be cross if he comes home and sees you like that!'

'What a cheeky young rascal,' said Holmes. 'Now, Jack, is there anything you would like?'

The boy thought for a moment. 'I'd like a shillin',' he said.

'Here you are, then. Catch! A fine child, Mrs Smith.'

'Bless you, sir, he is, but almost too much for me to manage when my man's away.'

'Away, is he?' said Holmes, sounding disappointed. 'That's a shame. I wanted to talk to Mr Smith.'

'He's been away since yesterday morning, sir, and I'm beginning to worry.'

'I wanted to hire his steam launch.'

'Why, it's in the steam launch he's gone. That's what puzzles me

because there ain't more coals
in her than would take her to
Woolwich and back.'

'He might have bought more
coal somewhere down the river.'

'I doubt it, sir. It's expensive
buying small amounts.
Besides, I don't like that
wooden-legged man with
his fierce face.'

'A wooden-legged man?'

'Woke us up about three
in the morning, night
before last. He's been
before and my man was
expecting him.'

'How can you be sure it was him?'

'His voice, sir, I know his voice. "Shake a leg, matey," he said, and my man woke Jim, our eldest, and off they went. I could hear the wooden leg clackin' on the stones.'

'What was the name of the boat?'

'The *Aurora*, sir.'

'She's not that old green launch?'

'No, indeed. She's been fresh painted, black with two red streaks.'

'Thank you. I shall go down to the river and if I see Mr Smith

I'll tell him you are worried. A black funnel, you say?'

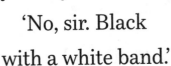

'No, sir. Black with a white band.'

'Ah, of course. Good morning, Mrs Smith.'

The lady curtsied and marched back inside, dragging her son after her.

'The main thing,' said Holmes as we crossed the river on a ferry, 'is never to let people know that their information is of the slightest importance to you. If you do they will shut up like an oyster. So, what would you do now?'

'I would engage a launch and go down the river on the track of the *Aurora*.'

'My dear fellow, that would be a huge task. There are so many wharves between here and Greenwich. It would take days to check them all.'

'Engage the police then?'

'No. I shall probably call Athelney Jones at the last minute. We must not let these men know they are being followed.'

'What are we to do then?' I asked
as we landed near Millbank Prison.

'Drive home, have some breakfast,
and get some sleep. We may be out
again tonight. We'll keep Toby, for
he may be of use to us yet. Cabby!
Stop at a telegraph office please!'

We pulled up at the Great Peter Street Post Office and Holmes sent a telegram.

'Whom do you think that was to?' he asked as we resumed our journey.

'I don't know.'

'You remember my Baker Street boys that we employed in the Jefferson Hope case?'

I nodded, laughing.

'This is just the sort of case where they will be useful. That telegram was to Wiggins. I expect he and his gang will be with us before we finish our breakfast.'

It was almost nine o'clock in the morning now, so I was feeling tired and my leg hurt. By this time the treasure was the one aspect of the case that held my interest. Part of it belonged to Miss Morstan and I was prepared to give my last ounce of strength towards recovering it for her, even though that would put her forever beyond my reach.

A bath and fresh clothes brightened me up considerably, and when I came down to the sitting room, our breakfast was laid and Holmes was pouring the coffee.

'Look at this,' he said, laughing as he pointed to the newspaper.

I took *The Standard* and read the short article.

8 d.

THE EVENING STANDARD

4th September 1888

MYSTERIOUS BUSINESS AT UPPER NORWOOD

At around twelve o'clock last night, Mr Bartholomew Sholto, of Pondicherry Lodge, was found dead in his room. There was no evidence of violence, but a valuable collection of Indian gems was missing.

The discovery was first made by Mr Sherlock Holmes and Dr Watson, who had called at the house with the brother of the deceased, Mr Thaddeus Sholto. Fortunately, Mr Athelney Jones of the detective police force happened to be nearby and was there promptly. His thorough investigation led to the arrest of Mr Thaddeus Sholto along with other members of the household.

The thieves had a good knowledge of the house. Mr Jones proved that they could not have entered by the door or the window, but must have made their way across the roof and through a trapdoor that led into an attic room above the deceased's bedroom.

'Isn't it wonderful?' said Holmes, grinning over his coffee.

'I think we are lucky not to have been arrested ourselves,' I said.

'So do I. I hope Jones doesn't have another attack of energy.'

At that moment there was a loud ring of the doorbell and I could hear Mrs Hudson raising her voice in dismay.

I rose from my chair. 'Holmes, I think they are really after us!'

'No. It's the unofficial force – The Baker Street Irregulars.'

As he spoke there came a swift pattering of bare feet on the stairs and in rushed a dozen street children. They formed a line, facing us. Then the tallest and oldest of them stepped forward.

'Got your message, sir,' he said, 'and brought 'em round as quick as I could.'

Holmes handed them three shillings and sixpence. 'In future they can report to you, Wiggins, and you to me. I want to find a steam launch called the *Aurora*, owned by Mordecai Smith. She's black with two red streaks and her funnel is black with a white band. She is downriver somewhere. I want one boy at Mordecai Smith's landing stage opposite Millbank to say if the boat comes back. You must search both banks thoroughly. Let me know the moment you have news. Is that clear?'

'Yes, guv'ner,' said Wiggins.

The Baker Street Irregulars
Very useful helpers. Wiggins and his gang have the freedom of the streets and know London well. They can observe, yet remain invisible. The usual rate of pay is a shilling a day, with a bonus of one guinea for the boy who finds a vital clue.
Mrs Hudson complains that they leave mud on the carpet.

'The old scale of pay, and a guinea to the boy who finds the boat. Here's a day in advance. Now off you go!'

'If the launch is above water, they'll find her,' said Holmes as they clattered down the stairs. 'They can go everywhere and see everything without being noticed. I expect to hear before evening.'

'Are you going to bed, Holmes?'

He shook his head. 'No, I'm not tired. I don't remember ever feeling tired by work, but idleness exhausts me completely. I am going to think over this strange business. Wooden-legged men are not so common, but the other man must be unique.'

'The other man again!'

'What do you think, Watson? Small footprints, feet never enclosed in shoes. Bare feet, stone-headed hammer, great agility, poison darts shot from a blowpipe.'

'South America,' I guessed.

He shook his head and reached to take a book off a shelf. 'This is the first volume of the most recent edition of the encyclopaedia. What have we here ...'

Little is known about the natives of the Andaman Islands beyond their physical appearance.

Their average height is under four feet and their feet and hands are markedly small. They are rumoured to use blowpipes when hunting.

'But how did he meet such an unusual companion?'

'Since Small came from the Andamans, it is not so strange. Look here, Watson, you look exhausted. Why not lie here on the sofa and try to get some sleep?'

He picked up his violin as
I stretched out on the sofa
and he began to play a
low, dreamy tune – his
own composition
I have no doubt.
I remember his
earnest face and
the rise and fall
of the bow. Then
I floated peacefully away
on a soft sea of sound until I
found myself in dreamland, with
the sweet face of Mary Morstan
looking down upon me.

When I woke late in the afternoon, feeling refreshed, Holmes was sitting in exactly the same position except that instead of his violin, he held a book.

'You have slept well,' he said. 'I was afraid our talking would wake you.'

'Is there news, then?'

He shook his head. 'Wiggins was here to report, but there is no trace of the launch. Every hour is of importance but we can only wait. If we leave here a message may come in our absence.'

'Then I shall run over to Camberwell and call upon Mrs

Forrester. She asked me to.'

'Only upon Mrs Forrester?'
Holmes asked with a twinkle in
his eye.

'Well, of course, Miss Morstan
too. I shall be back in an hour
or two.'

'Well if you are crossing the
river you may as well
return Toby. I don't
think we shall
have any more
use for him.'

I returned
the dog to
Mr Sherman,

along with a half sovereign, and
then continued to Camberwell,
where Mrs Forrester and Miss
Morstan were eager to hear
any news. I spoke of Mr Sholto's
death but left out the grimmer
details.

'It is a romance!' cried Mrs
Forrester. 'An injured lady, half a
million in treasure and a wooden-
legged ruffian.'

'And two knights to the rescue,'
added Miss Morstan with a bright
glance at me.

'Why, Mary, I don't think you
are excited enough! Just imagine

what it must be like to be rich and to have the world at your feet!'

It sent a thrill of joy to my heart that Miss Morstan showed no sign of pleasure at the thought. She gave a toss of her head as if the matter was of little interest to her. 'I am anxious for Mr Thaddeus Sholto, for he has been kind and honourable. It is our duty to clear him of this charge.'

It was evening before I arrived back at Baker Street and I was met by Mrs Hudson in the hall. 'Mr Sherlock Holmes has been acting strangely, sir,' she said.

'He's been pacing up and down and every time the bell went he came out to see who it was. I fear for his health.'

'I don't think you need worry, Mrs Hudson,' I reassured her. 'He has a small matter on his mind, which makes him restless.'

Nevertheless, I heard Holmes' dull tread, from time to time, throughout the night. I knew how frustrated he must feel at the delay.

At breakfast he looked worn and haggard. 'You are wearing yourself out,' I remarked.

'Yes, I could not sleep. This infernal problem is consuming me. The whole river has been searched on both sides, yet still there is no news.'

'Could it have gone upriver?'

'I have thought of that and sent a search party as far as Richmond. Surely we must soon hear something.'

But no word came all day. There were articles in most papers but no fresh details apart from that the inquest was to be held the following day.

The next morning in the early dawn I awoke with a start to find Holmes standing over me, dressed as a sailor with a thick woollen jacket and a coarse red scarf around his neck.

'I am off downriver, Watson. Please stay here in case any messages come, and take any action you think is necessary. Can I rely on you?'

'Most certainly.'

'You will not be able to telegraph me, for I do not know yet where my investigations will take me, but I hope I shall not be long.'

As I ate my breakfast, I read of further developments in *The Standard*.

We believe that the Upper Norwood Tragedy may be more mysterious than first supposed. Fresh evidence has shown that it is quite impossible that either Mr Thaddeus Sholto or his housekeeper could have had anything to do with the murder, so both were released yesterday evening. Further arrests may be expected any minute.

The Standard 7

I wondered what this fresh clue may be. Perhaps it was just

an excuse to cover up a police blunder. I was about to put down the paper when an article caught my eye.

MISSING: Mordecai Smith and his son Jim left Smith's wharf at about three o'clock last Tuesday morning in the steam launch *Aurora*, which is black with two red stripes, funnel black with a white band. The sum of five pounds will be paid to anyone who can give information to Mrs Smith at Smith's wharf, or at 221B Baker Street, as to the whereabouts of Mordecai Smith and the *Aurora*.

This was clearly Holmes' doing. It was clever, since the fugitives would not suspect anything but an anxious wife.

146

It was a long morning. Every time there was a noise outside I wondered whether it was Holmes returning or an answer to his advertisement. I tried to read but my thoughts kept wandering off. Could Holmes be stuck?

At three o'clock there was a loud ring of the bell, a booming voice in the hall and, to my surprise, Mr Athelney Jones entered.

He seemed very different from the brash and confident officer at Upper Norwood. Now he was meek and apologetic.

'Good day, sir,' he said.

'I understand that Mr Sherlock Holmes is out.'

'Yes, and I cannot say when he will be back. Perhaps you would care to wait? Would you like a drink?'

'Well, a small one. You know that I have been forced to reconsider my theory regarding the Norwood case? Mr Sholto was able to prove an alibi. From the time he left his brother's room he was never out of sight of someone. My reputation is at stake and I should be glad of some assistance.'

'We all need help sometimes,'
I said gently.

'Mr Sherlock Holmes is a
wonderful man, sir. I never saw a
case yet that he could not throw
a light on. He would make a most
promising officer. I have had a
telegram from him and understand
he may have a clue. Here it is.'

He handed me the telegram. It
was dated Poplar at twelve o'clock.

Go to Baker Street at once. If I
have not returned, wait for me. I
am on the track of the Sholto gang.
You can come with us tonight if
you want to see this through.

At that moment we heard a heavy step on the stair, with a great wheezing as if a man was struggling to get his breath. Once or twice he stopped as if the climb was too much for him, but at last he entered.

He was an old man with an old seafaring jacket buttoned to his throat. His back was bowed, his knees were shaky and his breathing was painfully asthmatic. He had a scarf around his chin and I could see little of his face except for a pair of keen eyes under bushy white brows, and long grey side-whiskers.

He looked about him slowly. 'Is Mr Sherlock Holmes here?'

'No, but can tell me any message you have for him.'

'It was to him I was to tell it,' he said.

'Was it about Mordecai Smith's boat?'

'Yes. I knows where it is. An' I knows where the men he is

after are. And I knows where the treasure is. I knows all about it.'

'Tell me and I shall let him know.'

'No, no. If Mr Holmes ain't here, he must find out for himself. I don't like the look of either of you.'

He shuffled towards the door but Athelney Jones moved to block him.

'Wait a bit, my friend,' he said. 'You have important information. We shall keep you here, whether you like it or not, until Holmes returns.'

The old man made a little

run for the door but realised
that it was useless. 'Pretty sort
of treatment, this!' he cried,
stamping his stick. 'I come here to
see a gentleman, and you two seize
me and treat me in this fashion!'

'Sit over there on the sofa,' I said,
'you will not have long to wait.'

He shuffled across to the sofa
sullenly and seated himself with
his face resting in his hands. Jones
and I resumed talking.

Suddenly, Holmes' voice
interrupted us. 'I think that you
might offer me a cigar too,' he said.

We both jumped. There was

Holmes sitting close to us with an air of quiet amusement.

'Holmes!' I exclaimed. 'You here! But where is the old man?'

'Here's the old man,' he said, holding out a heap of white hair. 'Here he is – wig, whiskers, eyebrows, and all. I thought my disguise was pretty good, but I hardly expected that it would stand that test.'

'Ah, you rogue!' said Jones, delighted. 'You would have made a good actor. You had that cough right, but I thought I knew the glint in your eye.'

'I have been working in this get-up all day,' said Holmes, 'You see, a good many criminals are beginning to know me so I can only carry out my investigations in disguise. You got my telegram?'

'Yes, that is what brought me here. But my case has come to nothing. I have had to release my two prisoners.'

'Never mind,' said Holmes,

lighting his cigar. 'I shall give you two others instead. You are welcome to all the official credit but you must do as I say. Is that agreed?'

'Entirely.'

'Well then, I shall want a fast police boat – a steam launch – to be at the Westminster Stairs at seven o'clock.'

'That is easily managed.'

'We will need two men in case of resistance.'

'There will be two or three in the boat. Anything else?'

'When we secure the men we

shall get the treasure. I think it would be a pleasure to my friend here to take the box round to the young lady to whom half of it rightfully belongs. Let her be the first to open it. Eh, Watson?'

'It would be a great pleasure to me.' I marvelled at how thoughtful Holmes could be sometimes, when at other times he seemed to have no regard at all for the feelings of others. It was strange that he could be both extremes at once.

'Rather irregular,' said Jones, shaking his head. 'However the whole thing is irregular, so

I suppose it will be all right. Afterwards the treasure must be handed over to the authorities until the official investigation ends.'

'Certainly. But one other point,' said Holmes. 'I would like to have information about this matter from Jonathan Small himself. You know I like to work the details of my cases out.'

'If you can catch him, I don't see how I can refuse you an interview with him. Anything else?'

'Only that I insist upon you dining with us.'

Our meal was a merry one.

Holmes could talk exceedingly well when he chose, and that night he did choose. He appeared to be in a state of nervous excitement. I have never known him so brilliant. He spoke on a wide range of topics - medieval pottery, Stradivarius violins,

warships of the future – handling each as though he had made a special study of it. Athelney Jones proved to be a sociable creature too. And I felt glad that we were nearing the end of our task so I was also in a good mood.

When we had finished, Holmes glanced at his watch and filled up three glasses with port. 'To the success of our little expedition,' he said. 'And now it is time we were off. Bring your revolver, Watson, and I shall bring mine. It is as well to be prepared. I see the cab is here.'

It was just after seven when we arrived at Westminster Wharf and found our launch waiting for us.

Holmes eyed it critically. 'Is there anything to mark it as a police boat?'

'Yes, that green lamp on the side.'

'Then take it off.'

After that was done, we stepped aboard and cast off. Jones, Holmes and I sat in the stern. There was one man at the rudder, one to tend the engines, and two burly police inspectors at the bow.

'Where to?' asked Jones.

'To the Tower. Tell them to stop opposite Jacobson's Yard.'

Our craft was a fast one. It shot past the long lines of loaded barges. Holmes smiled with satisfaction as we overtook a river steamer. 'We ought to be able to catch anything on the river.'

'Tell us how you found the *Aurora*,' I asked.

'My boys had been up and down the river without result. I knew that Small and his assistant had left the Smiths at three o'clock, and since Small's companion would be particularly noticeable, they couldn't get too far before daylight. They paid Smith to hold his tongue and reserved the launch for

their final escape, in a couple of days' time, once they saw that they were not under suspicion. Then they would go to Gravesend where they had no doubt arranged passage to America or the Colonies. But how could they hide the launch, yet have her ready for their escape when they wanted? I could only think of one way of doing it. Smith could hand the boat over to a boat-builder or repairer, with directions to make some small change. Then she would be taken to his shed or yard, and so concealed yet ready with only a few hours' notice.'

'That seems simple enough.'

'It is just these simple things
that are often overlooked. I
started in my seaman's outfit
and enquired at all the yards
along the river. At the sixteenth
– Jacobson's – I learned that the
Aurora had been handed over to
them two days ago by a wooden-
legged man, for repairs to her
rudder that were unnecessary.

'At that moment, who
should arrive but Mordecai
Smith, rather the worse
for drink and shouting

the name of the boat. "I want her at eight o'clock tonight," he shouted. They must have paid him well for he was chucking shillings about to the men. I followed him as far as an alehouse but then went back, found one of my boys and stationed him as sentry over

the launch. He is to stand by the water's edge and wave his handkerchief when they start. We shall be waiting for them.'

'You have planned it very well,' said Jones, 'but I would have had a body of police in Jacobson's Yard and arrested them when they came out.'

'Which would have been never. This man Small is a clever character. He would send a scout ahead and if anything made him suspicious he would lie low for another week.'

Meanwhile, we had been

shooting under the bridges that span the Thames. As we passed the City, the last rays of sun were just visible over St Paul's. It was twilight before we reached the Tower.

'That is Jacobson's Yard,' said Holmes, pointing to a mass of masts and rigging on the south bank. He took a pair of binoculars from his pocket and gazed at the shore. 'I see my sentry at his post,' he remarked. 'But no sign of the handkerchief.'

'Suppose we go downstream a little way,' suggested Jones, eager to be doing something.

'We cannot take anything for granted,' said Holmes. 'It's likely that they go downstream, but we cannot be certain. From this point we can see the entrance to the yard but they can't see us. We must stay here.'

Suddenly he was alert. 'Do I see a handkerchief? Surely that is a white flutter over yonder?'

'Yes, it is your boy!' I cried. 'I can see him.'

'And there is the *Aurora*!' exclaimed Holmes. 'And going like the devil. Full speed ahead, engineer. Make after that launch with the yellow light. By heaven, I shall never forgive myself if she proves to be faster than us!'

She had slipped out of the yard and passed between one or two craft so that she had built up speed before we saw her. Now she was flying downstream at a tremendous rate.

Jones shook his head. 'She is very fast,' he said. 'I doubt if we shall catch her.'

'We *must* catch her,' cried Holmes through gritted teeth. 'Heap on those coals, stokers. Make her do all she can.'

The furnaces roared and the powerful engines whizzed and clanked like a great metallic heart. Her sharp, steep prow cut through the still water and sent two waves rolling to left and right. With every throb of the engines our boat sprang and quivered like a living thing. One great yellow lantern on our bow threw a long, flickering funnel of light in front of us. Right ahead a dark blur upon the water showed where the *Aurora* was, and the swirl of white foam behind her spoke of the pace at which she was going.

We flashed past steamers

and merchant vessels. Voices
shouted at us from the darkness,
but still the *Aurora* thundered
on, and still we followed close
upon her track.

'I think we gain a little,' said
Jones with his eyes on the *Aurora*.

'I am sure of it,' said I. 'We
shall catch up with her in a few
minutes.'

At that moment, however, a tugboat blundered in between us. It was only with quick action that we avoided a collision, and by the time we had got round it the *Aurora* had gained a good two hundred yards. Our boilers were strained to the utmost and the frail shell creaked with the fierce energy that was driving us along.

We had shot past the West India Docks, down Deptford Reach, and up again after rounding the Isle of Dogs. We could now clearly see the *Aurora* and Jones turned the searchlight on her, so that we could plainly see the figures upon her deck. One man sat by the stern with something black between his knees. Beside him lay a dark mass of something. The boy held the tiller, while against the red glare of the furnace I could see old Smith, stripped to the waist and shovelling coals for dear life.

At Greenwich we were about
three hundred paces behind them.
At Blackwell about two hundred

and fifty. Never had sport given
me such a wild thrill as this mad,
flying manhunt down the Thames.
Steadily, we began to catch up,

yard by yard. In the silence of the night we could hear the panting and clanking of their machinery. We were close now. Jones yelled to them to stop.

At the sound of his voice, the man in the stern sprang up from the deck and shook his fists at us, cursing in a high, cracked voice. He was a powerful man and as he stood with his legs astride I could see that from the thigh downwards there was just a wooden stump on the right side.

At the sound of his angry cries, the huddled figure on the deck

moved. He was the smallest man I had ever seen, with a shock of dishevelled hair. He was wrapped in a blanket with only his fierce, angry face showing.

'We must have our revolvers ready,' said Holmes. 'If he raises his hand, fire.'

Even as we looked, the man plucked out a short, round piece of wood from under his blanket, and clapped it to his lips.

We fired.

The man whirled round, threw up his hands, and fell sideways into the river. I caught one glimpse of his furious eyes amid the white swirl of the waters.

At the same moment, the wooden-legged man threw himself on the wheel so that his boat made straight for the south bank, while we shot past her stern, only clearing her by a few feet. We were after her in an instant, but she was already nearly at the bank.

It was a wild and desolate place, where the moon glimmered on pools of stagnant water.

The launch ran up onto the mudbank with a dull thud. The fugitive sprang out but his stump instantly sank its whole length into the mud. He struggled, but could not take a single step either forward or backward. He yelled with rage and kicked frantically in the mud with his good foot, but his struggles only drove his wooden leg deeper into the soft ground.

We brought our launch up to the shore and threw a rope around his shoulders. Then we were able to haul him out over the side of our boat like some kind of evil fish.

The two Smiths, father and son sat sullenly in their launch but came aboard meekly enough when commanded. We hauled the *Aurora* off the beach and tied her to our stern. A solid iron chest of Indian workmanship stood upon her deck and I guessed that it must contain the treasure.

There was no key, but it was of considerable weight, so we transferred it carefully to our own little cabin.

As we steamed slowly upstream again, we flashed our searchlight in all directions, but there was no sign of Small's accomplice.

'See here,' said Holmes.

Just behind where we had been standing stuck one of those murderous darts. It must have whizzed between us the instant we fired. Holmes smiled and shrugged his shoulders, but I confess it turned me sick to think of the horrible death that had passed so close to us that night.

Our captive sat in the cabin opposite the iron box. He was a sunburned fellow, with lines and wrinkles all over his brown features. He had a large bearded chin and his age may have been around fifty, for his black, curly hair was streaked with grey.

His face was not unpleasant, although his heavy brows gave him a terrible expression when he was angry. He sat now with his handcuffed hands upon his lap while he looked with his sharp eyes at the box. It seemed to me that there was more sorrow than anger in his expression and he looked up at me with what seemed like humour in his eyes.

'Well, Jonathan Small,' said Holmes, lighting a cigar. 'I am sorry that it has come to this.'

'So am I,' he answered. 'And I give you my word that I never raised a hand against Mr Sholto. Tonga shot one of his darts into him. I had no part in it, sir.'

'How could you expect a small man like Tonga to hold Mr Sholto while you were climbing?'

'You seem to know as much about it as if you were there, sir. The truth is that I hoped to find the room empty. It was the time when Mr Sholto usually went down to supper. I am truly sorry about his death. I had no quarrel with him, only with his father.'

'You are under the charge of Mr Athelney Jones, of Scotland Yard.

He will bring you up to my rooms and I shall ask you for an account of the matter. You must be truthful about it, and then I hope I may be of use to you. I think I can prove that the poison acts so quickly that the man was dead before you ever reached the room.'

'That he was, sir. I got a fright when I saw him as I climbed in through the window. I would have been after Tonga but he ran off, leaving his club and some of his darts too, which I am sure helped put you on our track. I don't have any grudge against you, but it does seem ironic that I, who has a claim to half a million pounds, should spend the first half of my life building a sea wall in the Andaman Islands, and the other half in Dartmoor jail. It was a dark day when I first clapped eyes on the Agra treasure. It has brought a curse upon any man who owned it. To Major Sholto it brought fear and guilt and to me it has meant imprisonment for life.'

At that moment, Athelney Jones thrust his broad face and heavy shoulders into the cabin.

'Quite a family party,' he remarked. 'Well, I think we may all congratulate each other. I say, Holmes, you must confess that you cut it rather fine. It was all we could do to overtake her.'

'All's well that ends well,' said Holmes. 'But I certainly did not know that the *Aurora* was so fast.'

'Smith says she is one of the fastest launches on the river, and that if he had another man to help him with the engines, we never would have caught her. He swears he knew nothing of the Norwood business.'

'He didn't,' cried our prisoner, 'not a word. I chose his launch because I heard she was fast. We told him nothing but we paid him well.'

'Well, if he has done no wrong, we shall see that no wrong comes to him. Even though we are quick at catching our men, we are not quick in condemning them.'

Jones was already congratulating himself for the capture. I struggled to contain my laughter. From the slight smile that played over Holmes' face, I could see that the speech had not been lost on him either.

'We will be at Vauxhall Bridge soon,' said Jones, 'and I shall land you, Doctor Watson, with the treasure box. I need hardly tell you that I am taking a very grave responsibility upon myself in doing this. It is most irregular, but an agreement is an agreement. I must, however, send an officer with you, since you the treasure is so valuable. It's a pity that there is no key, so we may make an inventory first. You will have to break it open.

Where is the key, my man?'

'At the bottom of the river,' replied Small.

'You need not have given us the extra trouble. Doctor, be careful. Bring the box back with you to the Baker Street rooms. You will find us there, on our way to the station.'

They landed me at Vauxhall with the box with a friendly officer as my companion. A quarter of an hour's drive brought us to Mrs Forrester's. The servant seemed surprised at so late a visitor but explained that Miss Morstan was in the drawing room. I entered, box in hand, while the officer stayed with the cab.

She was seated by an open window. The soft light of a shaded lamp fell upon her as she leaned back in the wicker chair, playing over her sweet face, and tinting the rich coils of her luxuriant hair.

At the sound of my footsteps she sprang to her feet and a bright flush of surprise and pleasure coloured her pale cheeks.

'I heard a cab drive up,' she said, 'but I never dreamed that it might be you. What news have you brought me?'

'I have brought you something that is worth all the news in the world,' I said, putting the box upon the table and speaking cheerfully although my heart was heavy. 'I have brought you a fortune.'

She glanced at the iron box. 'Is that the treasure?' she asked, coolly.

'Yes, this is the great Agra treasure. Half of it is yours and half of it is Thaddeus Sholto's. You will have a couple of hundred thousand pounds each. There will be few richer young ladies in England. Is it not glorious?'

I think I must have been overacting, for she glanced at me curiously.

'If I have,' said she, 'I owe it to you.'

'Oh, no, not to me but to my

friend Sherlock Holmes. I could never have followed up a clue that has challenged even him. As it was, we very nearly lost it at the last moment.'

'Please sit down and tell me about it, Doctor Watson,' she said.

I explained briefly what had occurred since I had last seen her. Holmes' disguise, our expedition in the evening and the wild chase down the Thames. She listened with shining eyes. When I spoke of the dart that had so narrowly missed us, she turned so white that I feared she

was about to faint.

'It is nothing,' she said as I hastened to pour her some water. 'It is a shock to hear that I placed my friends in such horrible peril.'

'Then let us turn to something brighter,' I said. 'There is the treasure. What could be brighter than that? I thought it would interest you to be the first to see it.'

'It would be of the greatest interest to me,' she said, although there was little feeling in her voice. 'What a pretty box!' she added, leaning over it. 'This is Indian work, I suppose?'

'Yes.'

'And so heavy!' she exclaimed, trying to lift it. 'The box alone must be of some value. Where is the key?'

'Small threw it into the Thames,' I answered. 'I must borrow Mrs Forrester's poker.'

At the front of the box was a thick clasp. Under

this I thrust the end of the poker and twisted it outwards. The clasp sprang open with a loud snap and with trembling fingers I flung back the lid. We both stood gazing in astonishment.

The box was empty!

It was massive and well-made, but not one shred of metal or jewellery lay within it. It was absolutely and completely empty.

'The treasure is lost,' said Miss Morstan, calmly.

As I listened to the words and realised what they meant, a great shadow seemed to pass from my soul. I had not realised how much the Agra treasure had weighed me down until it was finally removed. It was selfish, but all I could think of was that the golden barrier had gone from between us.

'Thank God!' I cried.

She looked at me with a questioning smile. 'Why do you say that?'

'Because you are within my reach again,' I said, taking her hand. She did not withdraw it. 'Because I love you, Mary, as truly as ever a man loved a woman. Because this treasure sealed my lips. Now that it is gone I can tell you I love you. That is why I said, "Thank God".'

'Then I say "Thank God" too,' she whispered as I drew her to my side.

Whoever had lost a treasure? I knew that night that I had gained one.

Athelney Jones looked surprised when I got to Baker Street and showed him the empty box. Holmes lounged in his armchair with his usual thoughtful expression while Small sat opposite him with his wooden leg crossed over his other one. As I showed them the empty box he leaned back in his chair and laughed.

'This is your doing, Small,' said Jones, angrily.

'Yes. I have put it where you shall never lay hands upon it!' he cried. 'It is my treasure and if I can't have it, then no one shall. None of the four can have the use of it. I have acted for them as well as myself. The sign of the four, always. I know that they would have wanted me to do what I have done: throw the treasure into the Thames

202

rather than let it go to relatives of Sholto or Morstan. You'll find the treasure where the key and Tonga are. When I saw that your launch would catch us, I threw the loot into the river.'

'It would have been easier for you to have thrown the box and all,' remarked Jones.

'Easier for me to throw and easier for you to recover,' Small answered.

'The treasure is scattered over five miles or so.'

'This is a very serious matter, Small,' said Jones. 'If you had helped justice instead of thwarting it in this way, you would have had a better chance at your trial.'

'Justice!' snarled Small. 'Whose loot is this if not ours? Look how I have earned it. Twenty long years in that fever-ridden swamp, at work all day and chained up at night. Bitten by mosquitoes, racked with fever, and bullied by the guards. I would rather have one of Tonga's darts in my

side than live in a convict's cell
knowing that another man lives
in luxury with the money that
should be mine.'

All this was said in a wild whirl
of words while his eyes blazed
with fury and passion. I could
understand why Major Sholto was
so afraid when he learned that the
injured convict was on his track.

'You forget that we know nothing
of all this,' said Holmes quietly.
'We have not heard your story, and
we cannot tell how far justice may
have been on your side.'

'Well, sir, if you wish to hear

my story, I have no wish to hold it back. What I say to you is the truth, every word of it.' He took a sip of water from the glass beside him.

'When I was eighteen I joined the army. I was immediately sent to India and I had no sooner learned to handle a musket than I was foolish enough to go swimming in the River Ganges. A crocodile took me just as I was halfway across and nipped off my leg just above the knee.

Luckily, my company sergeant was in the water too and he saved me. I spent five months in hospital and was forced out of the army with this wooden stump, unfit for service.

'Well, I was twenty by then and down on my luck, but an indigo planter wanted an overseer to look after his employees and my colonel recommended me. The pay was fair and I had comfortable quarters so I was content, until a mutiny broke out. I stayed with the planter while the country was in a blaze around us.

'One day I was returning from a distant plantation and found my employer's bungalow in flames. I broke away across the fields with bullets whistling past my ears and late that night arrived safely within the walls at Agra.

'I joined a volunteer army, wooden leg and all, and eventually we moved across the river and took up position in the enormous old fort of Agra. It's a strange place. There's a modern part, which housed our troops, women, children, stores, and everything else. But the modern part is nothing like the old part. That's full of scorpions and centipedes in great deserted halls and winding passages twisting in and out. It's easy to get lost in it.

'The river washes along the front of the old fort and protects it, but on the sides and back there are many doors that had to be guarded. We were short-handed so it was impossible to have a guard on all of those doors. I was ordered to guard an isolated door on the south-west side of the building along with two Sikh troopers. I was instructed to fire my musket if anything went wrong, and help would come. Since there was a labyrinth of passages and corridors between us, though, I doubt they could have arrived in time to be of any use in an actual attack.

'Well, I was pretty proud of having this small command given to me. I was a new recruit, and a one-legged one at that. For two nights I kept watch with my troopers, Mahomet Singh and Abdullah Khan.'

Small took another sip of his water. I was fascinated by his tale and glad that Holmes had insisted on hearing it before Small was taken to the police station.

'The third night of my watch was dark, with driving rain. It was dreary work standing in that gateway hour after hour in such weather. At about two in the morning I took out my pipe and lay down my musket to strike a match. In an instant, the two Sikhs were upon me. One of them snatched my musket and aimed it at my head while the other held a knife

to my throat and swore he would
plunge it into me if I moved a step.

'My first thought was that these
fellows were in league with the
rebels. But even though I felt the

point of the knife at my throat, I opened my mouth with the intention of screaming, even if it was my last one.

'The man who held me seemed to know my thoughts and whispered, "Don't make a noise. The fort is safe enough. There are no rebels on this side of the river." I could see a spark of truth in the fellow's brown eyes so I waited in silence to see what they wanted.'

'"Listen to me, sahib," said the taller and the fiercer of the two, Abdullah Khan. "You must either be with us now or silenced forever.

Which shall it be – death or life? We can only give you three minutes to decide, for it must all be done before the guard does his rounds again."

"'How can I decide?" said I. "You have not told me what you want of me but if it's anything against the safety of the fort I'll not agree."

"'It is nothing against the fort," said he. "We ask you to be rich. If you join us, we will swear to you that you shall have your fair share of the loot."

"'But what is the treasure?" I asked. "I am ready to be rich."

"'You will swear then," said he, "to raise no hand and speak no word against us, either now or afterwards?"

"'I will swear it," I answered.

"'Then my comrade and I will swear that you shall have a quarter of the treasure that shall be equally divided among the four of us."

"'There are only three of us," said I.

"'No, Dost Akbar must have his share. Listen now, to what I have to say. There is a very rich raja in the northern provinces. When the troubles broke out, he made

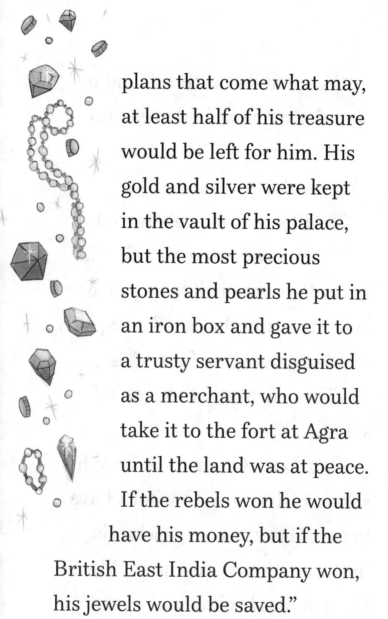

plans that come what may, at least half of his treasure would be left for him. His gold and silver were kept in the vault of his palace, but the most precious stones and pearls he put in an iron box and gave it to a trusty servant disguised as a merchant, who would take it to the fort at Agra until the land was at peace. If the rebels won he would have his money, but if the British East India Company won, his jewels would be saved."

'"This servant, who travels under the name of Achmet, is on his way to the fort. He has with him my foster brother, Dost Akbar, who knows his secret. He has promised to accompany Achmet to this gate. He will come here soon and he will find us waiting. The place is lonely and no-one will ever know Achmet was here. He will disappear and the great treasure of the raja shall be divided among us. What say you to this, sahib?"

'In England I would never have considered it but it is very different when there is fire and blood all around you, and you have been used to risking death at every turn. I thought about how my parents back in England would stare when they saw their son coming back with pockets full of gold.

'Thinking I was unsure, Abdullah Khan said, "Consider, sahib, if this man is taken by the governor he will be executed and his jewels will be taken by the government. The jewels will be as safe with us as with them. There are enough to make every one of us rich. Are you with us, or must we look upon you as the enemy?"

'"I am with you heart and soul," said I.

'He handed me back my musket. "You see that we trust you. We have now only to wait for my brother and the merchant."'

'"Does your brother know what you will do?" I asked.

'"The plan was his. We will go to the gate and share the watch with Mahomet Singh."

'The rain was still falling steadily. It was just the beginning of the wet season, and heavy clouds were drifting across the sky. It was hard to see more than a few yards ahead. A deep moat lay in front of our door, but in places the water had almost dried up so it could easily be crossed.

'Suddenly my eye caught the glint of a lantern on the other side of the moat. It vanished occasionally and then reappeared again, coming slowly in our direction.

'"Here they are!" I exclaimed.

'"You will challenge him, sahib, as usual," whispered Abdullah. "Give him no cause for fear. Have the lantern ready to uncover, so we may be sure that it is our man."

'I could now see two dark figures on the other side of the moat. I let them scramble down the sloping bank, splash through the mud, and climb halfway up to the gate before I challenged them.

'"Who goes there?" I said in a low voice.

'"Friends," came the answer. I uncovered my lantern and threw a flood of light upon them. The first was an enormous Sikh with a black beard that swept down to his waist. I have never seen so tall

a man. The other was a little fat, round fellow with a great yellow turban and a bundle in his hands, done up in a shawl. He seemed to be very nervous. His hands twitched and his head kept turning left to right, like a mouse when he ventures out of his hole.

'When he saw my face he gave a little chirrup of joy and came running towards me.

'"Your protection, sahib," he panted. "I have travelled far to seek the shelter of the fort at Agra. I have been robbed and beaten because I have supported the British East India Company. It is a blessed night when I am in safety – I and my poor possessions."

'"What is in the bundle?" I asked.

'"An iron box," he answered, "which contains one or two little family matters but which I should be sorry to lose. I shall reward you, and your governor also, if you will give me shelter."

'I could not trust myself to speak any more with this man. The more I looked at his fat, frightened face, the harder it seemed that we should slay him in cold blood. It was best to get it over with.

'"Take him to the main guard," said I.

'The two Sikhs closed in on either side with the giant walking behind as they marched in through the dark gateway. Then I heard a scuffle and footsteps coming towards me. I shone my lantern along the passageway, and there was the little fat man running faster than he'd ever run before, closely followed by the great bearded Sikh. As he approached, I stuck my musket between his legs and he tripped and rolled over twice. Then the big man was upon him.

'You see, gentlemen, I am keeping my promise and telling you everything,' said Small. He held out his manacled hands for the whisky and water that Holmes had poured for him.

I felt horror at the cold-blooded business in which he had been involved, and the careless way that he told the tale. He could expect no sympathy from me. Holmes and Jones sat with their hands on their knees and the same disgust written on their faces. Small might have noticed it, for there was a touch of defiance in his voice as he continued.

'It was all very bad, no doubt,' he said, 'but how many fellows in my shoes would have refused a share in the loot when they knew they would be killed if they didn't?

It was my life or his.'

'Go on with your story,' said Holmes, curtly.

'Well, we buried him in a corner by a crumbling brick wall. Then we went back to the treasure. A key hung from a silk cord near the handle on the top. We opened it and the light of the lantern gleamed upon a huge collection of gems. It was blinding to look upon them. When we had feasted our eyes we took them all out and made a list of them. There were hundreds.

'After we had counted the

treasure we put it back into
the chest and carried it to the
gateway to show Mahomet Singh.
We agreed to conceal our loot in
a safe place until the country was
at peace again and then to divide
it equally among ourselves. We
carried the box into the hall and
concealed it under some bricks
in one of the walls. We made
careful note of the place and
the next day I made four
maps and put the sign of the
four of us at the bottom,
for we had sworn that we
would always act for all. I

can say that I have never broken that oath.'

He paused to take breath again, looking round at us a little proudly.

'When peace came we hoped that we could safely retrieve our share of the plunder. But our hopes were shattered when we were arrested for the murder of Achmet.

It seems that the raja had sent
a second even more trusted
servant to spy on him, and when
he entered the fort and found no
sign of Achmet, a full search was
made and the body discovered.
Three of us were arrested because
we had been on watch at that gate
that night, and the fourth because
he had been in the company of
Achmet. We were all sentenced to
imprisonment for life.

'There we were with very little
chance of ever getting out while
a fortune waited for us outside.
It was enough to drive a man

mad. Then I was moved from Agra to the Andaman Islands. I was given a hut in Hope Town and was left pretty much to myself. There was digging and yam planting so we were busy enough all day. In the evenings we had a little time to ourselves so I learned to dispense drugs for the surgeon and picked up a little of his knowledge. All the time I was on the lookout for a chance to escape, but it is hundreds of miles from any other land.

'Sometimes the surgeon and other officers would meet to

play cards and I could often hear them talking while I made up the medicines. There was Major Sholto, Captain Morstan, Lieutenant Bromley-Brown, the surgeon himself, and two or three prison officials.

'Well, watching them play night after night, I noticed that the soldiers always lost.

Major Sholto was the hardest hit and began playing with huge sums of money. All day he would wander about looking as black as thunder.

'One night he lost more heavily than usual. I was sitting in my hut when he and Captain Morstan came stumbling along on the way to their quarters. "It's all over, Morstan," the major was saying. "I'll have to resign my post. I am a ruined man."

'That set me thinking.

'A couple of days later Major Sholto was strolling on the beach, so I went to speak to him.

"'I wish to have your advice, Major,' said I.

"'Well, Small, what is it?' he asked.

"'I wanted to ask you, sir. Who is the proper person to whom hidden treasure should be handed over? I know where half a million lies. I cannot use it myself, so I thought the best thing I could do would be to hand it over to the proper authorities. Perhaps they would get my sentence shortened for me.'

"'Half a million, Small?' he gasped, looking hard at me to see if I was in earnest.

"'Yes, sir, in jewels and pearls. It lies there ready for anyone.'

"'It belongs to government, Small, to government," he stammered, but I knew that I had got him.

"'Should I give the information to the Governor-General?" I asked, quietly.

"'Well, we mustn't do anything rash, Small. Give me all the facts.'

'So I told him the whole story,

with small changes, so he could not identify where the treasure was hidden. When I had finished he said thoughtfully, "This is an important matter, Small. You must not tell anyone about it. I shall see you again soon."

'Two nights later, he and his friend, Captain Morstan, came to my hut in the dead of night.

'"I wanted Captain Morstan to hear your story, Small," he said.

'I repeated it as I had told it before.

'"It rings true, eh? Good enough to act upon?"

'Captain Morstan nodded.

'"Look here, Small," said the major. "We have been talking it over and have come to the conclusion that this secret of yours is hardly a government matter, but a private concern of your own. Now, what price would you ask for it? We might at least look into it if we could agree to terms." He tried to speak in a cool, careless way, but his eyes were shining with excitement and greed.

'"Well, gentlemen," I answered, also trying to be cool. "I want you to help me secure my freedom, and do the same for my three companions. We shall then give you a fifth share to divide between you."

"'A fifth share, that's not very tempting," Morstan said.

"'It would come to fifty thousand each."

'"If only there were no others."

'"I must have the consent of my three comrades," I said.

'Morstan spluttered. "Nonsense! What have they to do with our agreement?"

'"They are in with me and we all go together."

'We had a meeting with Mahomet Singh, Abdullah Khan and Dost Akbar. At last we came to an arrangement. We would give both officers maps of the Agra fort and mark the place in the wall where the treasure was hidden. Major Sholto was to go to India

to test our story. He was to leave
the box where it was and send
out a small yacht where we four
could get to it. Captain Morstan
was then to apply for leave of
absence and meet us at Agra, then
we would divide up the treasure.
We swore an oath and I sat up all
night making the maps, signed
with the sign of the four.'

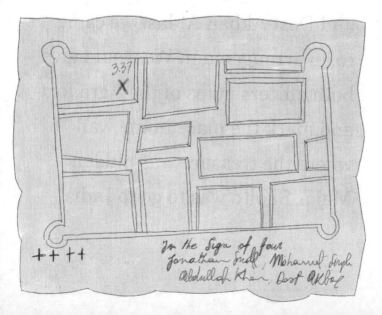

Small looked round at us again. 'Well, gentlemen, it is a long story and I know that Mr Jones is impatient to get me safely to the station. So I'll make the ending as short as I can. That villain Sholto went off to India but never came back. Morstan went over to Agra shortly afterwards and found, as we expected, that the treasure had gone. The scoundrel had stolen it all. From then on I lived only for vengeance. I thought of it day and night. To escape, to track down Sholto, to have my hands upon his throat – that was my one thought.

'Well, it was many years before my chance came. One day I met an Andaman Islander who was gravely ill. I took care of him and after a couple of months he got better. He took a liking to me and was always hanging about my hut. I learned a little of his language and that made him even fonder of me.

'Tonga was a fine boatman and owned a big roomy canoe. I saw my chance of escape, so I talked it over with

242

him. He was to bring his boat round to an old wharf that was unguarded, and pick me up.

'Tonga brought the boat as directed. After eleven days at sea we were picked up by a trader that was going to Jeddah. For a long time we drifted about the world until at last we arrived in England about four years ago. I had no trouble finding out where Sholto lived and set to work to discover whether he had spent the treasure or still had it. I soon found out that he still had the jewels. I tried to get him in many ways but he was pretty sly and always had two boxers as well as his sons to guard over him.

'One day I got word that Sholto was dying. I hurried to Pondicherry Lodge, mad that he should slip out of my clutches like that. I looked through the window

and saw him lying in his bed with his sons on either side of him. I'd have climbed inside and taken my chances with the three of them, but

he died right then before I could
do anything. I got into his room
that same night and searched
his papers to see if there was any
record of where he had hidden
our jewels. I found nothing, but I
scrawled the sign of the four and
pinned it to his chest.

'Tonga and I scraped a living,
and for some years there was no
news from Pondicherry Lodge
except that they were still looking
for the treasure. Eventually we
heard that it had been found in an
attic room above the laboratory.
I realised it was impossible for a

man with a wooden leg to climb
up there, although I knew there
was a trapdoor in the roof. I
went there with Tonga, who
could climb like a cat, and he
soon made his way in through
the roof. As luck would have it,
Bartholomew Sholto was still in
his room. Tonga thought he had
done something very clever in
killing him and was surprised

when I cursed him. I took the
treasure chest and lowered it
down on a rope I had brought. I
followed after leaving the sign of
the four upon the table to show
that the jewels had come back
to their rightful owners. Tonga
pulled up the rope, closed the
window, and made off the way he
had come, through the trapdoor.

'All this is the truth, gentlemen,

because I believe it's my best defence. I wish to tell the world how badly I have been treated by Major Sholto, and how innocent I am of the death of his son.'

'A very remarkable account,' said Holmes. 'A fitting end to an extremely interesting case. The only new information to me is that you took your own rope. I had hoped that Tonga had lost all his darts, yet he managed to shoot one at us in the boat.'

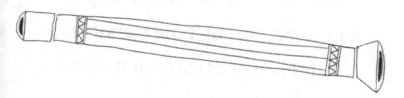

'He had lost them all, sir, except the one that was in his blow pipe at the time.'

'Ah, of course,' said Holmes. 'I had not thought of that.'

'Well, Holmes,' said Jones, 'you have heard Small's tale as you requested, but I shall feel more at ease when our storyteller is safely under lock and key. I am grateful to you both for your assistance. Of course, you will be wanted at the trial. Good night.'

'Good night, gentlemen,' said Small as they left the room.

'Well, there is an end to our

little drama,' I remarked after
we had sat in silence for some
time. 'And I fear that it is also an
end to our living arrangement,
Holmes. Miss Morstan has done
me the honour of accepting me as
a husband so we shall need to find
a home of our own. I am almost
recovered from
my injury and
hope to set up

my own medical practice.'

Holmes gave a dismal groan. 'I feared as much,' said he. 'I really cannot congratulate you.'

I was a little hurt. 'Have you any reason to be unhappy with my choice?'

'Not at all. I think she is one of the most charming ladies I have ever met. She has been most useful: she was very wise to preserve the Agra plan from her father's papers. But love is an emotional thing, and whatever is emotional is opposed to the reason that I place above all things. I shall never marry, in case I lose my judgement.'

'I trust,' I said, laughing, 'that my judgement may survive. But you look weary.'

'Yes. I shall be a limp as a rag for a week.'

'Strange,' I said, 'that such laziness alternates with your fits of energy.'

'Yes,' he answered, closing his eyes. 'I can be a very fine loafer and also a pretty lively sort of fellow.' He opened his eyes again. 'By the way, you heard that Small had an ally in the house – it must have been the butler. Jones actually managed to catch one genuine criminal as a result of all his arrests.'

'It seems rather unfair,' I remarked. 'You have done all the work, yet I get a wife out of it, and Jones gets the credit. What remains for you?'

'For me,' said Holmes, 'the satisfaction of having unravelled a great mystery.'

Sherlock Holmes

World-renowned private detective Sherlock Holmes has solved hundreds of mysteries, and is the author of such fascinating monographs as *Early English Charters* and *The Influence of a Trade Upon the Form of a Hand*. He keeps bees in his free time.

Dr John Watson

Wounded in action at Marwan, Dr John Watson left the army and moved into 221B Baker Street. There he was surprised to learn that his new friend, Sherlock Holmes, faced daily peril solving crimes, and began documenting his investigations. Dr Watson also runs a doctor's practice.

To download Sherlock Holmes activities, please visit www.sweetcherrypublishing.com/resources